CALENDAR CLUB MYSTERIES™

MYSTERY OF THE SNOW DAY BIGFOOT

by **NANCY STAR**

Illustrated by
JAMES BERNARDIN

SCHOLASTIC INC.

New York   Toronto   London   Auckland   Sydney
Mexico City   New Delhi   Hong Kong   Buenos Aires

For Gina and Linda
—N. S.

To Hannah, Payton and Harrison Clifton
—J. B.

ISBN 0-439-67262-7

12 11 10 9 8 7 6 5 4 3   5 6 7 8 9 0/0

Printed in the U.S.A.   40
First printing, January 2005

Book design by Jennifer Rinaldi Windau

CHAPTER ONE
SNOW DAY

LEON SPECTOR OPENED his eyes.

He looked at the clock on his night table.

It was seven-thirty in the morning.

He closed his eyes, crossed his fingers, and waited.

It came! Three long blasts from the firehouse siren.

That was how the Fruitvale schools let everyone know it was a snow day!

Leon looked out his window. He saw Dottie Plum waiting on her front walk.

Leon, Dottie, and Casey Calendar were best friends. They were also the first and only members of The Calendar Club.

Leon tried hard not to wake anyone up as he got dressed. He tiptoed past his parents' room. He tiptoed past the room where his little cousin, Stevie, was staying. He tiptoed down the stairs.

But when he got to the kitchen, he stopped.

The back door was wide open. A cold wind was blowing into the house.

Leon poked his head out the back door. But no one was there.

Then he saw them — footprints! And they weren't just any footprints. These footprints were gigantic. And they were heading straight toward his house.

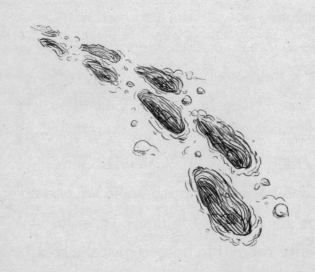

The front doorbell rang. Leon ran to answer it. It was Dottie and Casey standing on his front steps.

"Do you want to come out and play?" Casey asked.

"Yes," Leon said. "But I want to show you something first."

His friends followed him into his kitchen.

Leon pointed to the back door. "That was wide open when I woke up this morning."

"Did your dad leave it open when he left for work?" Casey asked.

"No," Leon said. "He's away on a business trip."

"Your mom probably left it open," Dottie suggested.

"No," Leon said. "She's just waking up now."

"Could it have been your cousin?" Casey asked.

3

Leon's little cousin Stevie was visiting for a week while his parents looked for a new house.

"Stevie was fast asleep when I came downstairs," Leon said. "I checked."

"I bet the lock is broken," Dottie said. "And the wind blew the door open."

"Maybe," Leon said. "But look outside."

Casey and Dottie went to the back window and looked out.

Dottie's eyes got wide. "Those footprints are huge," she said.

"Why are they coming toward your house?" Casey asked. Now Casey's eyes got wide. "Did someone come inside?"

"I don't think so," Leon said.

"Who has feet that big?" Casey asked.

"What are you looking at?" asked a small voice.

They turned and saw Stevie.

He had just woken up and he was still in his pajamas.

Stevie rubbed his eyes. "Can I see what you're looking at?"

Leon and his friends knew it wasn't a good idea for Stevie to look out the back window right now. He got scared too easily.

So Leon headed out of the kitchen. Stevie followed right behind him, like a shadow.

"Let's go out front," Leon said.

"What's in your backyard?" Stevie asked.

"Let's measure how deep the snow is on your front lawn," Dottie said.

"Is there something bad in the backyard?" Stevie asked.

"Hey, Stevie!" Casey said. "Do you want to help us make snow angels?"

"I'm in my pajamas," Stevie said.

"We'll wait while you get dressed," Leon said.

"Okay," Stevie said. And he raced upstairs to get changed.

As soon as he was gone, the three friends ran back to the kitchen. They looked out the window again.

The footprints looked even bigger than Leon remembered.

"Who made those footprints?" Casey wondered out loud.

"Why don't we meet in the clubhouse later," Leon said quietly. "Maybe we can figure out where those footprints came from then."

"What footprints?" a small voice asked.

Stevie was back. He had put his clothes on right over his pajamas.

"Come on," Casey said. "Last one out is a rotten egg."

Dottie, Casey, and Leon ran to the front door. Stevie followed.

Dottie got there first.

CHAPTER TWO
FOOTPRINTS!

DOTTIE LOVED TO BE first at everything. But one of her favorite things to be first at was making footprints in fresh snow.

Dottie made fresh footprints all over Leon's front lawn. It made her smile so much her teeth got cold.

Stevie stayed close to Leon's house. He looked worried.

"What's wrong?" Casey asked.

"What was in Leon's backyard?" Stevie asked again.

The three friends realized Stevie needed a little help to forget he was worried.

"Come on, Stevie," Casey said. "Want to make those snow angels now?"

"Okay," Stevie said. He still sounded worried, but he followed Casey to a fresh patch of snow.

They both lay down. They moved their arms and legs back and forth.

"Let's see what they look like," she said as she stood up.

"They look scary," Stevie said, still worried.

"Come on," Dottie called out. "Let's go measure the snow."

Dottie had brought a yardstick. She stuck it in the middle of Leon's snow-covered lawn. She put her finger on the spot where the snow touched the ruler. Then she pulled the ruler out.

"It's five inches deep!" she said.

She took her notebook out of her back pocket. Her notebook was where she kept lists. Her favorite list was of the weather.

"Today," Dottie's weather list said, "is our first snow day this year!"

She added another sentence: "Last night it snowed five inches."

"Was a bear in your backyard?" Stevie asked. "Warren Bunn told me there are big bears in Canada."

Stevie lived in Brooklyn, New York. But he was moving to Canada in the spring.

Warren Bunn was a boy in their grade who was a bully and proud of it.

"Why did you talk to Warren Bunn?" Casey asked.

"Because his sister is nice," Stevie said.

"Stevie played with Warren's little sister, Emma, yesterday," Leon explained.

"There are no bears in my backyard," he told Stevie. "Warren Bunn just said that to scare you."

"But are there bears in Canada?" Stevie asked.

Leon said he didn't know.

"Do you have a rock of Canada?" Stevie asked.

Stevie knew that Leon collected rocks in

the shape of states. He knew Leon hoped he'd have an entire map of the United States made out of rocks someday.

Stevie loved Leon's rock collection. He liked to look at the rocks every night before he went to bed. But he wasn't very good at geography yet.

Leon didn't mind.

"Canada isn't a state," he explained. "It's a country."

"Oh," Stevie said. "Warren Bunn told me it's so cold in Canada people wear boots all the time. Even to bed. He also told me there are giant moose with huge antlers, everywhere." Stevie thought for a minute. "Was there a moose in your backyard?"

"Hey, Stevie," Casey said. "Did you ever build a snowman?"

"Sure," Stevie said. "I've built lots of snowmen. I'm good at it. And I'm really

good at finding sticks for the arms. Did you
ever put boots on a snowman? I always
wanted to put boots on a snowman."

"Snowmen don't wear boots," Leon said.

"Why not?" Stevie asked.

"Snowmen don't have legs," Leon said.

"Why not?" Stevie asked.

Casey was famous for asking questions.
But Stevie asked more questions than
anyone they knew.

"I guess we could make a snowman wearing boots," Dottie said.

"Hey, Stevie," Casey said. "Do you want to be in charge of finding boots for the snowman?"

"Sure," Stevie said.

"I think we have some old boots in the garage," Leon said. "Why don't you go find them?"

"Okay," Stevie said. He ran off to find the boots.

Leon, Dottie, and Casey ran to the clubhouse. They didn't have much time before Stevie came back. But maybe it would be enough time to figure out who made the giant footprints in Leon's backyard.

CHAPTER THREE

PEANUT BUTTER, BANANA, AND BIGFOOT!

CASEY STOPPED IN FRONT of the Calendar Clubhouse to check the Help Box.

She had put the Help Box right outside the clubhouse front door. If anyone in Fruitvale needed help, all they had to do was slip a note inside.

The three friends checked the Help Box every day. They kept a tally sheet inside the clubhouse to keep track of their turns.

Today was Casey's turn.

She stuck her hand inside.

"There's something here," she called out to her friends.

They ran over to see what it was.

"Wait," Casey said. "It's not a note." She

pulled her hand out of the box. "It's a sandwich."

"Who would put a sandwich in the Help Box?" Casey asked.

Dottie sniffed it. "It's peanut butter and banana," she announced.

"That explains it," Leon said. "Peanut butter and banana is Stevie's favorite snack. I told him the Help Box is for notes. But he doesn't always listen."

"Look," Dottie said. She pointed to the bottom of the sandwich. "Something's stuck!"

Casey turned the sandwich over.

"It's a note!" she said. She pulled the note off the bottom of the sandwich and read it out loud: "Help! Bigfoot has come to Fruitvale!"

Casey looked for a signature but she couldn't find any. "Who's Bigfoot?" she asked.

"Bigfoot is the same as the Abominable Snowman," Dottie said.

"We learned about them when we studied legends," Leon said. "Remember?"

"No," Casey said. "Wait a minute. Did you learn about Bigfoot on the day I was home sick?"

Dottie nodded. "Yes. And that was the same day we learned about the Abominable Snowman and Sasquatch."

"What's Sasquatch?" Casey asked.

"It's a Native American word," Leon explained. "It means 'hairy giant.'"

"It's what they call Bigfoot in Canada," Dottie said.

"I'm moving to Canada," a voice said.

Stevie was standing behind them, holding a pair of big rubber boots.

He dropped the boots. "Are there hairy giants in Canada?" He sounded worried again.

"We found this in the Help Box," Casey said to change the subject. She held up the peanut butter and banana sandwich. "Is it yours?"

Stevie nodded. "I put it there for you. In case you got hungry."

"The Help Box is supposed to be for notes," Leon said. "Not for sandwiches."

"Sorry," Stevie said.

"Did you leave us this?" Casey asked. She showed Stevie the note they just found.

"No," Stevie said. "Are you mad at me about the sandwich?" He didn't like it when people got mad at him, especially Leon.

"No," Leon said. "We're not mad at you."

Stevie smiled. Then he remembered what he'd overheard. His smile turned into a frown.

"Is there a hairy giant in your backyard?" he asked.

"No," Leon said, hoping he was right.

"Are you sure?" Stevie asked.

"Hey, Stevie," Casey said. "Do you like brownies?"

Stevie nodded. He loved brownies.

"My mom makes the best double-fudge brownies in the world," Casey said. "And she might give us some if we make a really good snowman."

Stevie picked up the heavy boots he'd found in Leon's garage. "And I found really good boots. Can we make the snowman now?"

"Sure," Leon said, even though he really didn't want to.

Stevie could tell Leon wasn't acting like himself. "What's wrong?" he asked.

"Hey, Stevie," Casey said. "Do you want to go look for sticks to make the snowman's arms?"

Stevie nodded, and raced off to the back of Casey's yard. The evergreen trees there were so tall they made a canopy over the ground. There was a big area with no snow and lots of sticks. Stevie headed right for it.

Dottie, Casey, and Leon huddled together talking quietly.

"Who wrote that note?" Casey asked.

"Someone who thinks Bigfoot is real," Dottie said.

"Someone who thinks Bigfoot is in Fruitvale," Leon said.

"Is it possible Bigfoot is real?" Casey asked. "*Could* Bigfoot be in Fruitvale?"

"I don't know," Leon said. "But I do know that something with very big feet left very big footprints in my backyard."

"How big are Bigfoot's feet?" Casey asked.

"I don't know," Leon said again.

"We could find out," Dottie said. "If the library is open."

"I got the sticks," Stevie called out as he ran over. He had forgotten all about the hairy giant. So the three friends pretended they had, too.

CHAPTER FOUR

BIGGER THAN A GORILLA!

IT TURNED OUT THAT the snowman looked great with boots. And they all agreed. It was the best snowman any of them had ever made.

"Can we have brownies now?" Stevie asked when they were done.

"You can," Casey said. "But Leon, Dottie, and I are going to the library."

"Okay," Stevie said. "I'll come, too."

So Stevie and the three friends walked to town.

They were happy to see that the sidewalk in front of the library had been shoveled. The steps were cleared, too. That meant the library was open.

Dottie, Casey, and Leon led Stevie to the second-floor Children's Corner. They helped him pick out a big pile of books. Then they showed him where the cozy reading chair was.

Leon pointed to the long library tables where the older kids sat. "We'll be right over there. Okay?"

Stevie nodded and opened the first book.

The three friends walked over to Miss

Webster, the librarian. She was busy putting books on shelves.

"Do you have any books about Bigfoot?" Casey asked.

"Of course," Miss Webster said. She showed them where to look.

Dottie and Casey found two books right away. They carried them to one of the long tables. They sat and read for several minutes.

Dottie took out her notebook. She started a new page called, "Facts About Bigfoot."

"Write this," Casey said. She read from her book: "Bigfoot can be ten feet tall."

"That's even taller than my dad," Dottie said as she wrote. They read some more.

"My book says most people think Bigfoot is fake," Dottie said.

"My book says there's a lot of evidence

that Bigfoot is real," Casey said. "What does your book say, Leon?"

Leon didn't answer.

The girls looked up. Leon was nowhere to be seen. This was nothing new.

"Leon?" Casey called.

"Shh," Miss Webster hushed her.

Casey and Dottie got up. They walked up and down the aisles until they found Leon.

He was sitting on the floor. He had a book about states open on his lap.

This was nothing new, either.

"Why are you looking for facts about states?" Casey asked. "We're supposed to be looking for facts about Bigfoot."

"I found it," Leon said, pointing in the book.

"You found Bigfoot?" Casey asked.

"No," Leon said. "I found a picture of

Bigfoot. Actually, it's not a picture of Bigfoot. It's a picture of a statue of Bigfoot."

He showed the book to his friends.

"Does your book say Bigfoot is real?" Casey asked.

"Shh," Miss Webster said again.

The three friends went back to their table.

"This statue of Bigfoot is in the state of Washington," Leon explained. "Washington is one of the first states where Bigfoot was ever spotted. Some miners saw Bigfoot near Mount St. Helens, the volcano. After the volcano erupted, people said Bigfoot was killed."

"You mean even if Bigfoot did exist, now it's gone?" Casey asked. She sounded relieved.

Leon shook his head. "No. Because people who believe in Bigfoot don't think

it's just one creature. They think there are a lot of them. They think they might be like gorillas, only a lot bigger."

"Listen to this," Dottie said, looking in her book. "Some people report that the feet of a Bigfoot are twice the size of adult human feet. They can be as long as nineteen inches."

"How big are the footprints in your backyard?" Casey asked.

"I don't know," Leon said.

"How big are our footprints?" Casey asked.

"I don't know," Leon said again.

"I could measure them," Dottie said. "But I left my ruler in the clubhouse."

"Then the clubhouse is where we should go," Casey said.

They were just outside the library when Leon remembered Stevie.

He ran back to get him.

"Come on, Stevie," he called.

"Shh," said Miss Webster.

"Where are we going?" Stevie asked as he ran out of the library after his cousin.

"We're going to get you some brownies," Leon said. He didn't mention that while Stevie was eating brownies, the Calendar Club was going to measure the big, scary footprints in Leon's backyard.

CHAPTER FIVE
BIGGEST BIGFOOT EVER!

LEON TOLD STEVIE he had to stay in the kitchen to eat his brownie so there wouldn't be crumbs.

Then he and his friends went to his room to measure their feet.

Dottie started a list called "Foot size."

She wrote as she measured.

"Leon's feet are five inches long," she wrote. "Casey's feet are five and a half inches long."

She measured her own feet. "My feet are five and three quarter inches long."

Dottie finished recording their foot sizes. Then they went out to the backyard.

Dottie had to measure the giant footprints twice because the first time

she didn't believe it.

"Twenty inches long," she said as she wrote it down.

"Do you know what that means?" Casey asked. She didn't wait for anyone to answer. "Not only could these prints be from Bigfoot, they could be from the biggest Bigfoot ever."

Foot size

Leon's feet are five inches long.

Casey's feet are five and a half inches long.

My feet are five and three quarter inches long.

Giant footprints are twenty inches long!

"A monster-sized Bigfoot," Dottie said.

"A monster?" a voice said.

It was Stevie. He was standing very close to the house. He was staring at the footprints. And he was scared.

"Come on," Casey said. "Let's have a snow race. They're so much fun!"

Stevie was still scared. But he didn't want to miss out on something fun.

"What's a snow race?" he asked.

Casey didn't know what a snow race was. She had just made it up. But she quickly figured it out.

"In a snow race," Casey explained, "you stand in the snow and spin around in a circle really fast. And when you get too dizzy, you fall down. The last person to fall down wins. Do you want to try it?"

"Please, Stevie," Dottie said. "It won't be fun unless you do it, too."

"Okay," Stevie said.

It was the first-ever Calendar Club Snow Race. Dottie spun around and fell down first. Leon spun around and fell down second. Casey fell down third. Stevie fell down last and won.

When the first-ever Calendar Club Snow Race was over, Leon's backyard was completely covered with their footprints. And Stevie forgot all about the monster that had stomped through the backyard.

CHAPTER SIX

THEY'RE BACK!

TWO DAYS LATER Leon woke at exactly
7:30. His room looked brighter than usual.

Three short blasts came from the
firehouse siren.

It was another snow day!

Suddenly, Leon heard a banging noise. It
was coming from downstairs.

He jumped out of bed. He peeked into his parents' room. His mother was fast asleep. His father was still away.

He peeked into the room where Stevie slept. Stevie was fast asleep, too.

He raced downstairs to the kitchen.

The back door was wide open. It banged against the wall. A cold wind blew into the house. And then he saw it: a large packed snowball on the kitchen floor.

Leon walked to the back door and poked his head outside.

The backyard was covered with a fresh coating of snow.

The first-ever Calendar Club Snow Race footprints were gone.

But the giant footprints were back. And they were heading straight for Leon's house.

The doorbell rang.

Casey and Dottie were waiting on his front steps.

"Can you come out and play?" Casey asked.

"The footprints are back," Leon said.

The girls ran with Leon to the kitchen. He showed them the snowball, the door, and the footprints.

"When did you make that snowball?" Casey asked.

"I didn't make it," Leon said.

They went to the window and looked out.

"The footprints go from the driveway to your house," Dottie noticed.

"But where did they start?" Casey asked. "They seem to come out of nowhere."

They were trying to come up with an explanation for this when Leon's mother came into the room.

"The kitchen door was open again," Leon told her. "There's a big snowball on the floor. And there are more giant footprints in the backyard."

Mrs. Spector looked at the snowball and the door and the footprints.

Then she called Officer Gill.

He was there in five minutes.

Officer Gill bent down and touched the snowball. It was starting to melt.

"That's snow," he said.

"We know," the three friends said together.

He walked to the back door. He opened and closed the lock. He turned the knob. "It doesn't seem broken to me," he said.

"We know," the three friends said again.

Officer Gill opened the door and looked outside. "Those are mighty big footprints."

"Did the monster come again?" a voice asked.

Everyone turned. It was Stevie. He had just woken up and was rubbing his eyes.

"Well," said Officer Gill. "I don't know who made those footprints. But I do know there are no monsters in Fruitvale."

He peered through the window. "Someone's been out there, though. Someone's been out there for sure."

Officer Gill told Mrs. Spector to get a new lock for her back door.

Leon picked up the melting snowball and put it in a bowl. He thought Officer Gill might want it for evidence.

Then the three friends went to the clubhouse to see if anyone else had seen Bigfoot and left them a note during the night.

CHAPTER SEVEN

THE IVY-COVERED HOUSE

"THERE'S A NOTE!" Dottie said when she checked the Help Box. She opened it up.

"It's from your mother," she told Casey.

Casey took the note and read it aloud:

"Dear Calendar Club,

Mrs. Miller called to ask if you could shovel her front walk.

Can you help her?

Love, Mrs. Calendar."

"We don't have anything else planned this afternoon," Dottie said.

"And while we're out shoveling, maybe we'll see some other neighbors," Leon said.

"And we can ask them questions," Casey

said. "Like if they've seen anything unusual in their backyards."

"Something hairy," Leon said.

"Something big," Dottie said.

"Let's go," Casey said.

They got their shovels and set out for Mrs. Miller's front walk.

But they hadn't gotten very far when a voice called out, "Wait for me."

It was Stevie, running to catch up.

"Shoveling is hard work," Leon told him. "Maybe you should stay home."

Stevie stuck out his lower lip. His eyes got teary. It was how he always looked when he was about to cry.

Leon didn't want him to cry. "Or you could come along and help."

Stevie's frown turned into a smile so big it took up half his face.

Mrs. Miller's front walk was not very long. But it still took a long time to shovel.

After they were done, they took their shovels and walked up the block looking for neighbors to talk to.

But no one was outside. It was quiet except for Stevie's nonstop talking.

"What state do you want to find next?" he asked Leon.

Leon thought for a minute. He thought about the Bigfoot statue. "Washington," he said. "I'd like to find the state of Washington."

"What is Washington famous for?" Stevie asked.

"I was once at Uncle Eddy's store when he got a big shipment of apples from Washington," Dottie said.

Dottie's uncle owned a fruit and vegetable store that sold lots of apples, and other things, too.

"They were really good," she added.

"Washington is famous for its apples,"

Leon said. "In fact, the apple is Washington's state symbol."

"Does Washington have a state brownie?" Stevie asked.

"I don't think so," Leon said.

"Does Canada have a state brownie?" Stevie asked.

Leon sighed. Sometimes he got tired of all of Stevie's questions.

Leon glanced across the street, and stopped walking. "Look!"

The three friends looked.

They were across from the ivy-covered house at the corner of Daisy Lane.

The ivy-covered house was usually dark.

The woman who lived there was hardly ever home.

When she was home, she stayed inside.

Dottie, Casey, and Leon couldn't be totally sure the woman in the corner house didn't like kids. But they were pretty sure.

They did not like to walk in front of the ivy-covered corner house. They always crossed the street to avoid it when they went to town.

It was a Calendar Club superstition.

But today the woman in the ivy-covered house was home. And she was outside shoveling her walk.

The woman wore a big puffy coat. The puffy coat had a big puffy hood. The hood was pulled up over her head. It covered half her face.

"Who is that?" Stevie asked.

"A neighbor," Dottie said. She didn't want Stevie to get scared again. "She's hardly ever home."

"We don't know why," Casey said.

"She doesn't have any kids," Dottie said.

"We don't know her very well at all," Casey said.

Leon wasn't saying anything. He was

just staring.

"What are you staring at?" Casey asked.

"Her feet," Leon whispered. "Look at her feet."

They looked.

The woman's puffy coat was long. But sticking out from the bottom were her boots. And they were big. They were very big.

"Her boots are huge," Dottie said.

"They're enormous," Leon said.

"Do you think those boots could leave twenty-inch footprints in the snow?" Casey asked.

The woman across the street stopped shoveling. She turned toward Casey, Dottie, Leon, and Stevie.

"Come on," Casey said. She grabbed Stevie's hand and started running.

"Where are we going?" Stevie asked.

"Home," Leon said.

"Why are we running?" Stevie asked.

"It's another race," Dottie said.

She ran as fast she could. But this time, she let Stevie get there first.

CHAPTER EIGHT

THE SUSPECTS

DOTTIE, CASEY, AND LEON sat on the clubhouse floor. Dottie's notebook was open to a new list called, "Footprint Suspects."

So far all it said was, "Bigfoot!"

"Are you going to add 'the woman in the ivy-covered house'?" Casey asked.

"Yes," Dottie said. And she did.

"I don't think she's the one," said Leon.

"Why not?" Casey asked. "Did you see the size of her boots?"

"They looked big enough to make those footprints to me," Dottie said.

"She might be strange," Leon said. "But I don't think she would go into my backyard. Or put a snowball in my kitchen."

"She might," Dottie said. "If she wanted to scare you."

"Leon might be right," Casey said. "Why would she want to scare him?"

"Maybe she wanted to scare Stevie," Dottie tried.

"Why would she want to scare Stevie?" Casey asked.

"Maybe he asked her too many questions," Dottie said.

"That could be," Casey said. "Because you know how sometimes when Stevie asks questions, he doesn't wait for an answer? He just asks another question? And then another one? And then another one?"

Dottie and Leon looked at Casey. Then they laughed.

Casey frowned. "Do you think I ask too many questions?"

"No," Leon said.

"Do you think the woman in the corner house might be trying to scare me?" Casey asked.

"No," Leon said. "We don't even know if her feet are big enough to make those footprints."

"And I don't think any of us wants to ring her bell and ask for her shoe size," added Dottie.

"We don't have to do that," Casey said. She took Dottie's notebook and flipped to the page marked "Foot size."

"I have an idea," she said. "We can go to her house tonight after dark." She moved closer and whispered, "We can look for a set of her footprints in the snow. And we can measure them."

The three friends agreed this was a good plan.

They had an early dinner. It was just starting to get dark when they went out. But it wasn't too dark for measuring.

Casey led the way down the shoveled sidewalk. She carried a flashlight.

Dottie followed behind, holding the ruler in one hand. In the other, she had her cat, Ginger's, leash. Ginger was a cat who thought she was dog. She didn't bark or growl. But she did like to go for walks on a leash.

Leon came last, with Stevie. Stevie held Leon's hand so hard it hurt. Leon had tried to convince him to stay home. He told his cousin they were going to take care of some Calendar Club business that would be very boring.

But after Stevie listened, he stuck out his lip the way he did before he was going to cry.

So Leon took Stevie along.

"It's dark," Stevie whispered to Leon as they walked.

They were almost at the corner house.

"That's because it's almost night," Leon said. He tried to sound brave.

"Where's the moon?" Stevie whispered. He looked up at the sky.

Leon looked up at the sky, too. Stevie was right. The moon was not out. That made it even darker.

They came to the corner house. Casey stopped. Dottie and Ginger stopped. Leon and Stevie stopped.

There were no lights on in the corner house. It looked like no one lived there.

"Is it time for us to go home?" Stevie asked.

"Not yet," Leon said.

Casey pointed her flashlight to the sidewalk. She looked for a footprint to measure. But the woman in the corner house had done a good job shoveling. There were no footprints in sight.

Casey led the way to the end of Daisy Lane, pointing her flashlight ahead of them. They turned up the side street, onto

Appleton Road. But the woman in the corner house had done a good job shoveling there, too.

They walked a little farther. Then Casey stopped. "I found some," she called out in a whisper.

She pointed the flashlight to a set of footprints leading up the driveway to the woman's backyard.

The footprints were very big.

Dottie gave Ginger's leash to Leon. Then she walked up to the spot where the footprints started. She bent down and carefully measured. She wrote the number down in her book.

"Okay," she said when she was done. "Let's go."

The three friends, Ginger, and Stevie hurried down Appleton Road.

But when they got back to the corner of Daisy Lane, Stevie stopped.

"What's that?" he whispered. He pointed toward the corner house and toward the low iron fence that went around the house.

It was too dark to see clearly. But they could make out shapes on the fence. Then they heard voices.

"I'm scared," Stevie whispered.

"It's okay," Leon said. He didn't want to make Stevie nervous. But Leon was a little bit scared, too.

CHAPTER NINE
GHOST STORIES!

THEY HEARD A LAUGH.

"I know one that's even scarier," a voice said.

"It's Warren Bunn," Dottie whispered.

"Superb," said a different voice.

"That's Derek Fleck," Leon whispered.

Their eyes adjusted to the darkness. They could see clearly now. Warren Bunn and his best friend, Derek Fleck, were sitting on the iron fence.

There was only one reason to sit on the iron fence in front of the corner house. That was to tell ghost stories.

"Bigfoot," Warren called out in a loud, scary voice. "Bigfoot is coming."

Derek laughed so hard he snorted.

That made Warren laugh, too.

Casey marched over to them.

"Warren Bunn," she said. She sounded mad. "Did you leave a note about Bigfoot in our Help Box?"

Warren stopped laughing.

"What if I did?" Warren said. "Can't you take a joke? You didn't think it was real, did you?"

Now Casey was really mad. "Did you make those footprints in Leon's backyard?"

"Footprints?" Warren said. "What are you talking about?"

"She's talking about the giant footprints in my backyard," Leon said.

"Is that your idea of a joke, too?" Casey asked.

"I don't know anything about giant footprints," Warren said. "Except that I didn't make them."

"I don't believe you," Leon said.

"Why should we believe you?" Casey said.

"Because he's telling the truth," Dottie said.

"What do you mean?" Casey asked. "How do you know?"

"Warren couldn't have made those footprints," Dottie said. "And neither could Derek. They fell in the snow yesterday. They both hurt their ankles. My mom told me."

"We didn't fall in the snow," Warren said. "We crashed our sleds. On purpose."

"Both of them have casts on their feet," Dottie said. She took Casey's flashlight and pointed it toward Warren. They could see the small cast on his left foot. She pointed it toward Derek. His right foot was in a cast, too.

"If Warren and Derek made those footprints, we would have seen marks from their crutches in the snow," Dottie said.

"Good going, Sherlock," Warren said.

He picked up his crutch and waved it in the air. "Big whoop to you."

"What are you doing here, anyway?" Derek asked.

"I bet I know," Warren said. "I bet they're out looking for rocks. In the snow. At night. That's how smart they are."

Leon ignored the comment. "Okay," he said to his friends. "So Warren left the note. But he didn't make the footprints or leave the snowball."

"And the woman in the ivy-covered house didn't make the footprints either," Dottie said. "See?" She showed her friends the page where she wrote down the measurements of the woman's footprints in the snow. "Her footprints are eleven inches long. That's all."

"Then we're back where we started," Leon said.

"Back to Bigfoot," Dottie said.

"What are you talking about?" Warren asked.

"You know that note you put in our Help Box?" Casey asked.

"Yeah," Warren said. "What about it?"

"It turns out you're right," Dottie said. "We think Bigfoot has come to Fruitvale."

"What?" Warren said.

"There are giant footprints in my backyard," Leon said. "And they're not human. They're too big to be human."

"But they're just the right size to be Bigfoot's," Dottie said.

"Can you believe they think that stupid stuff about Bigfoot is true?" Derek asked Warren. He laughed and snorted again.

But this time Warren didn't laugh along. He stood up, grabbed his crutch, and hobbled down the sidewalk toward his house.

"Wait for me," Derek yelled. He hobbled after him.

"You made that up to scare them away, right?" Stevie asked as he watched the two boys disappear into their houses.

"No," Leon admitted. He didn't want Stevie to be scared. But he didn't want to lie to him, either.

"I think I want to go home now," Stevie said.

Dottie, Casey, and Leon wanted to go home, too.

They ran all the way to Leon's house.

Dottie got there first.

As soon as they were inside, Stevie went upstairs to change into his pajamas.

Dottie, Casey, and Leon went into the kitchen to have a snack.

That's when Leon noticed the bowl on the kitchen counter.

"Look at this!" he said.

"What is it?" Casey asked.

"It's a bowl filled with water and rocks," Dottie said.

"Why did you put rocks in a bowl of water?" Casey asked.

"I didn't," Leon said. "I put a snowball in that bowl. And the snowball melted into water."

"Then where did the rocks come from?" Casey asked.

"They must have been inside the snowball," Leon said.

He took three small rocks out of the bowl. They were gray, wet, and shiny.

"How did rocks get in a snowball?" Casey asked. "How did the snowball get in your house?"

"I don't know," Leon said. "Just like I don't know who left my back door open. Or who made the footprints in my backyard."

"I have an idea," Casey said after a moment, "for how we can find out."

CHAPTER TEN

KEEPING WATCH

IT TOOK SOME CONVINCING, but
Casey got Mrs. Spector to agree. The three
friends would have a sleepover. They would
spend the night in sleeping bags in Leon's
living room.

They promised to get ready for bed early.

They promised they wouldn't stay up
late talking.

And if they heard anything strange, they
promised to let Mrs. Spector know.

Stevie asked if he could sleep in the living
room with them, too. But Stevie's parents
were coming the next day. So Mrs. Spector
said he had to be well rested. That meant
he had to sleep upstairs.

"Why?" Stevie asked.

Mrs. Spector told Stevie they could talk
about it once he was in bed.

As soon as Stevie was upstairs, Dottie, Casey, and Leon settled into their sleeping bags.

Then they got ready to stay awake all night.

Staying awake turned out to be harder than they expected. So they decided to take turns.

Dottie went first.

She told Leon she would wake him up as soon as she felt tired.

After fifteen minutes, Dottie felt a little sleepy. But it was too soon to wake up Leon. So she closed her eyes, just for a second. That's when she accidentally fell asleep.

The house was silent. Then a noise startled Dottie. She sat up.

"Leon," she whispered.

She heard another noise.

"Casey," she whispered.

Leon and Casey's eyes popped open. They sat up, too.

They all heard it. It was the sound of footsteps. They were coming closer.

Their eyes adjusted to the darkness. Then they saw him. It was Stevie!

"What are you doing?" Leon asked Stevie.

"Wamganna," Stevie said.

"What did he say?" Casey asked.

"Bomganna," Stevie said. He had a funny look on his face. It was as if he didn't see them.

Stevie slowly walked to the kitchen.

Dottie, Casey, and Leon followed him.

Stevie went to the small room off the side of the kitchen where Leon's family kept their coats and shoes.

He picked something up.

"What is he doing?" Casey asked.

Leon watched his cousin. "He's carrying

boots," he said. "A pair of my father's really old boots. He must have found them in the garage this morning."

"Stevie, did you take those boots from the garage?" Casey asked.

Stevie just stared.

"Why won't he answer us?" Casey asked.

"He can't," Dottie said. "He's not awake."

"What do you mean?" Casey asked.

"He's sleepwalking," Dottie said.

"How can you tell?" Casey whispered. "He looks awake."

"He's not," Dottie said. "My brother used to sleepwalk when he was little. He used to get all ready for school while he was asleep. Once he even went outside and sat on the front steps to wait for the bus. My mom used to walk him right back to bed. And when he woke up in the morning, he didn't remember a thing."

Casey turned to Leon. "Has Stevie ever sleepwalked before?"

"I never heard about it," Leon said. "Stevie?"

"It's as if he can't hear you," Dottie said. "That's what it was like for my brother, too. He did it a lot. And then one day he just stopped."

"Stevie?" Leon said again.

Stevie didn't answer. He opened the back door. He put on Leon's father's boots.

"Where is he going?" Casey asked.

He stepped outside.

"What is he doing?" Casey asked.

The boots were very heavy and big. Stevie dragged his feet as he walked.

"Look," Leon said.

"He's leaving footprints!" Dottie said.

"And they're huge!" Casey said.

It was true. The boots were so heavy that Stevie left enormous footprints with every step he took.

"It's not Bigfoot who's in Fruitvale," Casey said. "It's Stevie!"

Stevie dragged his feet, making giant footsteps all the way to the driveway. Then he bent down. They couldn't see what he was doing.

But when he was done he turned around and walked back in the same footsteps. This made the footprints even bigger.

He got to the house and stopped.

"What he's doing now?" Casey asked.

They couldn't tell. But a moment later he was finished. He opened the door and walked into the kitchen. He sat down and pulled off the boots. He put them back in the room with the shoes and coats.

Then he put something in the middle of the kitchen floor.

"It's a snowball!" Dottie said. "That's what he was doing. He was making a snowball!"

"Why?" Casey asked. "Why would he make a snowball and bring it into the house?"

"It's like he left a little present," Dottie said.

"That's exactly what it is," Leon said. "It's a present."

They watched Stevie walk out of the kitchen. They heard the creak of the stairs as he walked back to bed.

Leon picked up the snowball. He carried it to the sink. He turned on the water and held the snowball under the faucet.

In a few seconds, the water made the snowball start to melt. Leon held it under the faucet until the snowball was all gone. And all that was left of it was what Stevie had put inside. Rocks.

"He was digging in the gravel driveway," Leon explained. "He was looking for rocks for my collection. And look what he found," Leon said, holding up a rock.

Dottie and Casey came closer.

"What is it?" Casey asked.

"It's Washington," Leon said. "Stevie accidentally found a rock shaped like the state of Washington!"

Leon put Washington in his pocket. Then he went to wake his mother.

CHAPTER ELEVEN
NOT A SNOW DAY!

STEVIE'S PARENTS ARRIVED in time for lunch. Mrs. Spector invited Casey and Dottie to join them.

"I sleepwalked?" Stevie asked his cousin and his friends. "For real?"

"For real," Leon said.

"And we wouldn't have known about it if not for the Calendar Club," said Stevie's mother.

Dottie, Casey, and Leon beamed.

"They thought I was a hairy monster," Stevie said. "But I wasn't. I was just me."

Everybody laughed.

Stevie's mother told them that she'd called Stevie's doctor. He said Stevie's sleepwalking would probably go away soon. In the meantime, they would put new locks on all the doors.

"We have a lot of doors in our new house in Canada," Stevie boasted.

After lunch, it was time for Stevie to go. But Leon had something for him.

It was a box. The box was small but heavy.

Stevie opened it right away.

Inside was a rock.

"What is it?" Stevie asked.

"It's a rock of Texas," Leon explained. "I found it in the driveway in the same place you found the rock of Washington."

"I found Washington," Stevie boasted.

"I already have a rock of Texas," Leon explained. "But I thought you might want to start your own collection."

"Maybe I can find a rock of Canada, too," Stevie said.

"Maybe," Leon said.

"Hey, Stevie," Casey said. "Do we have time for one last snow race?"

Stevie's parents agreed. There was

enough time for the second-ever Calendar Club Snow Race.

Dottie spun around and fell down first. Leon spun around and fell down second. Casey fell down third. Stevie fell down last and won.

Stevie got into the car. The three friends waved until the car was out of sight. They had to admit that Stevie could be very annoying. But they missed him already.

That night it snowed ten inches at Stevie's new house in Canada.

But in Fruitvale it didn't snow at all. In the morning, the Fruitvale firehouse siren did not go off.

It was a regular day.

Bigfoot was not in Fruitvale.

And Dottie, Casey, and Leon were happy to finally go back to school.

The Monthly Calendar

~~~~~~ Issue Three • Volume Three ~~~~~~

JANUARY

Publisher: Casey Calendar
Editor: Dottie Plum
Fact Checker: Leon Spector

Snow Day Bigfoot

In January, Fruitvale School had its first snow day of the year. But even though school was closed, the Calendar Club stayed open. Someone needed to figure out who was making those giant footprints in Leon's backyard!

Dottie measured them. They were bigger than any human foot could be. Was someone trying to scare the Calendar Club? Was someone trying to scare Leon's little cousin, Stevie? Or was it true that Bigfoot had come to Fruitvale?

Calendar Club members Dottie Plum, Casey Calendar, and Leon Spector stayed up all night to figure it out. And everyone was surprised at what they found!

DOTTIE'S WEATHER BOX

This January it snowed three times in Fruitvale. It snowed two inches on January 1st (Dottie's birthday!). It snowed fives inches on January 3rd. It snowed four inches on January 5th. It rained on January 20th. How many inches of snow fell in all?

ASK LEON

Do you have a question about a state for Leon Spector? If you do, send it to him and he'll answer it for you.

Dear Leon,
I love dinosaurs and I love fossils. Is there such a thing as a state fossil?

From,
I Love Fossils!

Dear I Love Fossils!,
I love fossils, too! And you're not the only one who wished there was a state fossil. Students in an elementary school in the state of Washington wanted a state fossil, too. And they got one! Washington's state fossil is the Columbian Mammoth!

Maybe your state has a fossil, too. If it doesn't, you could try to get your state to name one! If you're successful, let me know!

Your friend,
Leon